420 CHARACTERS

❋ 420 CHARACTERS ❋

STORIES

LOU BEACH

HOUGHTON MIFFLIN HARCOURT
BOSTON   NEW YORK
2011

For my mother, Emily Lubicz

For information about permission to reproduce selections from this book,
write to Permissions, Houghton Mifflin Harcourt Publishing Company,
215 Park Avenue South, New York, New York 10003.

www.hmhbooks.com

Library of Congress Cataloging-in-Publication Data
Beach, Lou.
   420 characters : stories / Lou Beach.
      p. cm.
   Summary: "The debut fiction project of an acclaimed artist and illus-
trator, 420 CHARACTERS is a collection of sharp and evocative min-
iature stories first presented as Facebook status updates"—Provided by
publisher.
   ISBN 978-0-547-61793-0
   I. Title. II. Title: Four hundred twenty characters.
   PS3602.E226A15 2011
   813'.6—dc22   2011009143

Book design by Melissa Lotfy

Printed in China

SCP 10 9 8 7 6 5 4 3 2 1

The stories you are about to encounter were written as status updates on a large social networking site. These updates were limited to 420 characters, including letters, spaces, and punctuation. The author hopes you enjoy them.

THE STORM came over the ridge, a rocket, dropped rain like bees, filled the corral with water and noise. I watched lightning hit the apple tree and thought: "Fritters!" as we packed sandbags against the flood. There was nowhere to go that wasn't wet, the squall had punched a hole in the cabin roof and the barn was knee-high in mud. We'll bury Jess later, when the river recedes, before the ground turns hard again.

THE TRAIN pulled into the station. I hesitated before stepping down to the platform, then made my way to the shoeshine stand. I sat, put my foot up on the metal rest. The old man looked up before tending to my shoe. "You new in town?" I told him that indeed I was. "OK then," he said and began cleaning my loafer. There was a local paper on the chair next to mine. The headline read: FIRE IN HOSPITAL MELTS IRON LUNG.

ZUMA PEDLEY hailed from Lubbock, came to L.A. in '02 with his guitar, some songs, and an ugly dog. He didn't think to change the world, wasn't built that way, but thought music might lessen the burden of those with hearts. He was looking for an army of smiles, but settled for a girl with corn hair and a bungalow in the hills, grew tomatoes. The dog is still ugly.

I AM EXPLORING in the Bones, formations of caves interspersed with rock basins open to the sky. I hear a sound like a turbine as I exit a cave and approach the light ahead. I'm sure it's a waterfall. What I encounter is a massive beehive, honeycomb several stories high, millions of bees. I crouch down to avoid detection and notice a shift in the tone of the hive's collective drone. I turn around and see the bear.

SHE TRUSTED grins, they were shot directly from the heart. Whereas smiles, oh, smiles could trick, be untrue, do you harm. Mendacious, twisted with bad intentions, like her father's, his mouth turned up at one corner like a beckoning finger, pulling his eye down into a squint.

WHILE I WAS AWAY you managed to rust all my tools. How is that possible? Did you dip them in the bathtub like tool fondue? I do not understand. You deny everything but cannot explain the rusted brad puller, pliers, awl, and bucksaw in our bed. "Maybe someone was playing a joke," you say, then add: "A wet hammer is still a hammer."

THE GUNNYSACK hangs from the pommel, full of sparked ore. I let Shorty sip from the stream, long neck arching in the sun. There is a ghost in the cottonwood I sit under to reread your letters. It tries to sniff the pressed flowers you sent from the garden in Boston, but the scent is gone. The petals and paper, envelope, all smell like campfire now.

MOUSE AND I lie on our stomachs on the warm and weathered planks. The little bridge spans the stream two feet below and the sun lays its hands on our backs. We drop pebbles into the creek and startle water striders, add to the trove of shining rocks and stones. Preteen bombardiers, we laugh at splashes. Twenty feet away, in another world, our parents and their friends sit on blankets, eat sandwiches and drink beer.

HE CALLED AGAIN. I accepted the charges of course, paid no attention to what he was saying, it's always the same story. I focused on the background noise — the grunts and rough laughter, the shouting. Once I heard a scream, his receiver clattered against the wall, the line went dead. I picture the wall, men leaning against it, scratching names and pictures into it, waiting for their turn. I try to imagine the smell. I can't.

TODAY I'M JIMI HENDRIX, but I don't own a guitar so I set fire to a kitchen chair instead. The crowd roars. My wife refuses to be the drummer, just clucks and stirs the soup. "Have some bisque, Hendrix," she says, hands me a bowl then sits down at the table. I have to stand, 'cause I burned my ax, man. So cool, so cool.

LORD MUMFORD cleared the table with a sweep of his arm. Before the clattering pewter had come to rest, the dogs were fighting over the gristle and bits of potato, lapping after rolling peas. "Brandy!" he shouted and pounded on the table. Sunday Pringle stood before him with decanter and glass. Mumford put his fat hands on her slim hips. "Stop trembling," he said.

THERE IS A KNOCK AT THE DOOR. Another. I slip out of my house shoes and Indian-creep to the peephole. I peek and see only hair, shiny dark. I hold my breath. There is banging on the door. I crouch, duck-walk to the couch and lie down behind it, perfectly still. I close my eyes. There is a knock on the door across the hall.

HUMANITY SERVICES came around today. They checked on the size of our bed, the quantity of cans in the pantry, the amount of stretch in your panties. I wasn't home at the time, it was my shift at The Mill, and you were at work, but Angie let them in. They inspected her hair and teeth, measured Buddy's doghouse. Angie said they were polite. She offered them a glass of water but after testing our faucet, they declined.

THE MUSEUM GUARD smiles as I shuffle past the familiar paintings to the one in the corner, near the fire extinguisher. It is a picture I myself painted long ago, when I was very young. It baffles me, I don't understand it. Why did I paint it? I stand before it until closing time, looking for clues, knowing I'll return tomorrow to look again.

CLIFF KNODES had a thin mustache, clusters of wisps that faded as they swam across his upper lip and met at the philtrum. At thirty he expected a more hirsute profile, a pistolero smear above his mouth. He applied nostrums, oils, and unguents, all to no avail, remained pink, fuzzy as a skinned bunny. He met a woman whom he convinced to forgo the waxing she maintained for years. He loved the scratch when they kissed.

I HAD NEVER punched anyone in the face before and was surprised at how much it hurt my hand. I wrapped a bag of frozen peas around it to take down the swelling. My father, the recipient of the blow, held a piece of raw steak, hurriedly taken from the freezer, against his black eye. Our relationship thus thawed, we pressed cold cans of beer to our foreheads, promised to meet again in the future for further bashing.

"ARE YOU MY MOMMY?" said the little blue egg. "No, dear. You are a plastic trinket full of sweets," said the brown hen. "My baby is over there," and she pointed to a pink marshmallow chick being torn apart and devoured by a toddler. The hen screamed and woke up, her pillow wet with sweat, the sheets twisted around her legs. "Christ, I hate that dream." She reached for a smoke.

NOT FAR FROM HUNTSVILLE we waited. Johnny and I whittled on some birch, but Messenger paced the river, said he was leaving if Del didn't show up soon. I told him to calm down, check the guns, make sure the rope wasn't tangled, see there was enough room in the trunk. He threw me one of his chickenshit looks, spit in the water, but pretty soon he was sitting on a rock practicing his knots, good boy.

THE BOOK SITS IN MY LAP, heavy and dull as cinder block. Why he chose me, I don't understand. I did not know him. Perhaps he saw my photo in the paper, was impressed with my philanthropies, or the cut of my jib. It arrived the day after he was found floating in the bay. It was wrapped in brown paper, festooned with stickers and hand-drawn stars, tied with twine. It smelled of cigarettes. There was postage due.

HE DIDN'T tie his shoes the way the other kids did. He had his own method. And though sometimes the loops of his tying attempts were longer than the dangles, he never lost a shoe when running from the bullies. The shoes were always brown, leather soles, metal eyelets, shined. He walked everywhere until he was given a bicycle as a graduation gift, pedaled out of town on Saturday, told his mother he was going bowling.

I BRING Copernicus to the vet's office and this guy is standing there, his thumb swathed in bandages. The doctor comes out carrying a large cage that contains a beautiful macaw, its belly wrapped in gauze and tape. He hands the man the cage, then reaches into his lab coat, brings out a small box. He offers it to the bandaged man. "Some of it was already digested, but here's what we could save."

THE WANKER IN THE WARDROBE sits on my wife's shoes. He amuses himself by pressing his face into her wool skirt. He breathes deeply, imagines himself a bat flying through a humid night. Each evening we leave a saucer of gin out for him. One time we panicked when the dish remained untouched for three days. He'd been away.

"OPEN THE GODDAM DOOR, RONNIE! I mean NOW!" He's locked himself in there again, turned Slayer and Deathhammer up all the way, the cheap speakers distorting the already distorted to the point where I know the fish will pulsate and wobble in their water. The blue tetras Miriam got him after his release, to make the room cheery. The poor, poor little fish.

THE OAK TABLE, set for twelve with bone white china and crystal goblets full of sparkling water, glistening silverware, was sprouting lettuce. It pushed out of the worn wood, knocked over the glasses, spilled water that irrigated the new growth. Plates were overturned by root vegetables pushing upward, silverware sent scattering by tomato vines and beanstalks until the entire table was a victorious garden.

HE FISHED the Pecos, sat on the bank singing about Jesus and crows, card games and shootouts. He ran out of songs, hoped the river wouldn't run out of fish. Peeling off his boots, he stepped into the water, shouted the name of a girl who married a grocer, didn't want to ride or plant corn or pull a calf out of a cow. He shouted her name till his throat was raw, then drank from the river and lay down on a rock to dry.

THE FLOOR MANAGER cued him for the break. "When we return, a report on elder abuse." He stood and stretched, sat back down when the stylist came to fix his makeup, adjust his hair. "You're so handsome," she whispered as she dropped two pills into his waiting hand. "You're killing me," he said and put his hand on her ass.

THE PRISONER OF NOISE stood before the bathroom sink, fingers in his ears, head down, mouth wide open, willing the sounds in his head to spill into the basin — the yelps and booms, screeches, screams and howls, crashes and groans, explosions and roars and babel and bangs. What if they formed a hairball of din, clogged the sink, scared the children when they came in at night to pee? He closed his mouth, went back to bed.

"MY LIFE IS NOT some cheap reality show, a magazine spread," she said, crossing her legs. I pushed myself away from the table, stood up and looked around at the other loungers sunning themselves at the café. "You know, Vivian, you should get a website, sell those things you make. I bet there's a market for them." She ground her cigarette into the ashtray, finished her wine. "Maurice, you are such an idiot."

THERE WAS A MOUSE that lived behind the big metal trash can in the kitchen. Mother weighed the can's lid down with a brick to forestall rodent encroachment. She wrapped a piece of twine around it, tied it to the handle at the center of the lid. One day she returned from the mill to find the twine chewed through. The brick lay on the linoleum, looking guilty.

TURNS OUT she wasn't really pregnant, just doing a number, needing someone to hold onto. Hell, I've been married four times, I sussed it out. Anyways, I cut her loose in Bismarck and got a job on a road crew. Saw a big gray wolf deep in a field of snow. He sniffed the air and was gone.

"GERONIMO!" I leap from the trestle high above the river, imagine myself parachuting into occupied France during WWII and meeting up with Marie, a beautiful dark-haired fighter of la Résistance. We kill some Krauts together, then hide out in the hayloft of a barn. I draw her to me, kiss her neck, her full red lips, unbutton her tight white blouse, and hit the cold water. "Sacrebleu!" I scream. "Sacre fuckin' bleu!"

I SAW YOU on the road, in the distance. You were walking to town holding Kim's hand. I couldn't reach you, there were wolves between us, they were sleeping, their teeth hidden, but their tails twitched and I was afraid. I took the back way to town and searched for you in the fog. Someone whispered that you were at the hotel and I went there, but all the doors were locked. I slept under a bush and waited for you.

THE LOOK ON THE NURSE'S FACE when she scanned my chart should have told me to stay put, but I was determined to march out of that ward and into the street and back to Flaherty's. No one said a word as I hoisted myself onto the barstool, barefooted, my ass hanging out of the back of the hospital gown.

FREEDOM, peaceful roamer, sniffer of trash and trees, catcher of thrown balls, a real good mutt, was shot by my jerk neighbor Norris, a mean prick who'd chop up your ball with an ax if it landed in his yard. Freedom wandered onto Norris's land and Norris popped him with the .22 rifle he uses on squirrels. We had to amputate Freedom's left hind leg, but he's a better three-legged dog than Norris is a two-legged human.

THE ASPEN SHIMMERED like the flank of a trout as I made my way down through the foothills and into the meadow. The bay whinnied and scared up some grouse. We stopped at the stream and I dismounted, let her drink. I wiped the inside of my hat, lay down in the grass, and read the clouds until my eyes closed and I dreamed of the sea.

THE SCHOOLGIRLS marched through the snow, melted it with their youth, heads haloed in heat. They felt secure within their green coats, silver crosses hanging from white necks. He stood behind a tree and pared his fingernails with a buck knife, wondered if the clippings would root in the soil beneath the snow and burst forth in spring as fingers that would clutch the ankles of those who strayed from the path.

I DON'T KNOW HOW she tracked me from Bismarck. Maybe she followed my scent. Anyway, I was working in Waukesha putting up vinyl siding and I look down and there she is, looking up at me with a hand on the ladder. "Hey." "Hey." I was still a little pissed at that pregnancy bullshit she tried to pull, but there was something about the curve of her neck and that dumbass gap-toothed grin . . .

THE ROWBOAT drifted into the cove dragging an oar, scoring wake through the green water. The name *Buttercup* was painted on the prow in bright blue, but the outline of a former name was still visible — *False Wind.* The boat bumped up against the pier and a black lab came running to meet it, wagging its tail until it saw that nothing was aboard but a pocket watch on the seat, hot from the sun.

NOT MUCH TO DO in town, never was, really. Since the plant closed and the Chevy dealer moved to Hadley, May's is only open on weekends and for breakfast, three fat old farmers arguing about the same thing for twenty years over gummy omelets. Jimmy and I covered the water tower with gang signs, dirty words, smoked reefer while we watched town from above. Teen gods. It's time to leave. Hello, Bloomington!

THE HOUSE was tucked into the bottom of a cul-de-sac, surrounded by a high brick wall. One of the bricks was missing and in the cavity lived a tiny man, Ray. He shared the space with a finch, a lovely lady from Indiana, Jill. She often gave Ray rides to the drugstore so he could pick up his medication, and he in turn constructed a nest for Jill out of cotton from his prescription bottles. There was no hanky-panky.

I'M ALONE ON DECK, sharing a smoke with myself. There's no moon but the stars are a city in the sky and I can see for miles. A last puff and I flick the cigarette over the rail and watch it spin in the wake, succumb. I raise my eyes and catch a dimple at the horizon, where the sea tucks itself under the sky. It's home, half a pack away.

HUEY "PUDGE" WILSON, county sheriff, never met a man he didn't like to handcuff. What he knew about law wouldn't fill a thimble but what he knew about power would overflow the rain barrels between here and the river. Justice was just a tool of power, meted out in back rooms and measured in bruises and broken bones. When he was found slumped over in the cruiser, dead, Happy Hour took on new meaning.

MUD. I pick it from between the hounds' toes, scrape it off Henry's flank. I leave my boots on the porch, go in, sit by the cherry piece. It's got the radio on it, Jesse's picture, and a shot glass Ma got at a casino downstate. She keeps a little blue stone in it that I found in the creek when I was four, gave her a delight when I presented it to her. She puts her finger in there and touches it sometimes.

FROM THE RIDGE, the stand of trees in the valley below looks like a hairbrush, left behind, perhaps, by an itinerant giant on his way to Delaware or Pennsylvania or one of those eastern states, where he'll crush hamlets and scare the populace. Here in The West the only giants are the mountains and the spaces between, enormities that can crush a man who merely beholds them. "Be humble," they moan, "beware, be humble."

THOUSANDS OF STARLINGS pulled the lo-
comotive through the sky swollen, the color of new
bruises. Above Lake Erie they faltered and fell,
cracked against the frozen gray water. The great
black engine listed and plunged headfirst, berserk
icebreaker, past startled pike, cowcatcher impaled in
silt, underwater obelisk, smoke-filled bubbles rising.

FOR-EV-UH. She had it tattooed in a little arc over her left boob, like a military patch. She'd punch me in the arm, punctuate each syllable, leave a blue mark. Told me that's how long her love would last, shouted it out. After a few months she seemed distant, took off one night for Tulsa with the drummer from a hair band. I went to Skin'N'InK, asked Mooney if he could make me a tattoo of a bruise, put it up on my arm.

I DON'T CARE MUCH FOR PLUCKY HERO-
INES. I do have a soft spot for hard types and wait-
resses and divorcées. Which is why I like Reno, I
guess. I can hopscotch and hobnob, bourbon in hand,
from lounge to coffee shop to poolside. The Rogaine
is saying "Harvest time!" and the Viagra fills me with
that can-do spirit. I'm on fire, baby!

HOOVES clattered and slipped on the rocks. We struggled up the dry wash, climbed past walls of baked mud, fallen trees, until we got to a rise over-looking a valley ringed by mountains. A waterfall plumed into a river that meandered through mead-ows and sparse woods. You rose high in your stir-rups, the wedding gown bunched around your waist. "Oh, it's a cup of Heaven all right," you said and rode whooping down the hill.

I SECURE THE HOUSE, plywood over the doors and windows, cancel the electric and phone, the worthless paper, the heating oil. Last time I shipped out, I had Ronnie and June watch the place, take care of things. But they broke up and neither can be trusted on their own, so now I just board the house up and forget about it until I'm home again. Time goes by onboard ship and when I return the weeds look the same.

I LOOKED down at the spots on the pavement where kids waiting for the bus had dropped wads of gum for years. The sun had seared them black, fried them flat. This concrete constellation held a secret that I knew could be unlocked. I went home and returned with a jar of paint and brush, connected the dots. A pattern emerged. I will share it with you. Be on the no. 12 bus at midnight, corner of Wrigley & Hubba Bubba.

HE SPLASHED bourbon into the coffee in his cup, went out to retrieve the morning paper. It lay in the grass, soggy, the sun still too sleepy to lap up the dew. Tire tracks embroidered the edge of the lawn. On the porch, in the old rocker, he tried to recall what he'd done the night before, whom he'd seen, how he got home. Someone flushed the toilet inside and he panicked, spilled his drink. "What a waste," he said.

I KISS your neck, the sweet spot behind the jaw where your ear lays its shadow. A curl of your hair catches in my mouth and I sputter and cough. You laugh, push me away and continue dusting the room, ask me to get a fresh bag for the vacuum cleaner. I go to the hall closet, return to find you sitting on the couch, naked. You look up at me, smile. You are pinning back your hair. "I don't want you to choke," you say.

HE FOLLOWED HER around the store, attracted by a certain rumpity thing, the gap between her two front teeth, her colors. He passed her quickly, hoped the movement of air would fetch him a scent, then returned, slow, gave her the shy guy smile. She smiled back, held his gaze until he turned away, nervous, made as if to read the label on a can of beans, put stuff in his cart, hurried to the checkout and out to the Kia.

"DON'T take the road with the ruts," says Santos. He flicks the safety, puts the gun back in the desk. The barrel is hot from all the shooting, and I imagine the papers in the drawer — the phone bill, the market coupons, the report card — catching fire, the desk and Santos going up in flames, the pens in his shirt pocket melting into his chest. And I'd be off the hook. "Get going," he says and throws me the keys.

DANNY AND I stand outside the church, fidget in our muted plaid sport coats. Maybe not muted enough. An old guy in a tuxedo walks up to Danny and hands him some car keys. "What's this?" says Danny. "Aren't you the parking valet?" says the guy. "No, I'm the best man." The guy walks away and we see him later inside. He's the father of the bride. "Oh, it's going to be a fun reception," Danny says, taking out the flask.

THE BEAUTIFUL YOUNG WOMAN waves at me across the plaza. I wave back and approach her, realize too late that she was waving at the man behind me. I open my mouth to speak as they embrace, kiss, and look deep into each other's eyes. I stand alone, surrounded by the festive crowd, feel old and foolish. I buy a postcard to send to my wife and children in Ohio. "Having a great time. Wish you were her."

THE DOG eyed us from the doorway. We passed quickly, my uncle covered in dust from the explosion. I held his hand, the same one that showed me how to repair a fishing net, that put a sweet in my pocket. The other hand held a cell phone that kept ringing. We passed through the market, into alleys that lead to the wilds, never looked at anyone. At the river, he glanced at the phone, shrugged, threw it into the water.

I'VE NEVER SEEN who lives across the street in the house with the peeling paint, broken steps. The shades are always down and the mailman rarely stops there, no paper is delivered. Only in winter is there any sign of activity. Every day the snow behind the chainlink fence is peppered with birdseed and the yard is alive with sparrows and finches, chickadees and dark-eyed juncos.

CHEAP AND GAUDY as jellybeans, hard as a jawbreaker, Candy Nelson sat on the bench in front of Jessops Hardware, filing her nails. Discomfited by yet another yeast infection, she crossed and uncrossed her legs, finally just opened them like a book, displaying to the illiterate Luther Choate, driving by, a page from heaven, causing him to lose control of his pickup and run over a red hound that was crossing the road.

I KEEP MY FRIENDS IN A BOX under the bed, categorized and separated, secured by blue rubber bands that originally held broccoli. One day I removed the lid and saw that they had all turned into little bones. I strung them together into a long strand that I looped around and around my neck.

THEY ARE CLOSING THE MINE in two weeks, they say. Six days a week bumping down in the gondola, pecking out the rocks and hauling them back up, doing it again the next day for twenty-seven years, one cave-in, three thin raises, and a failed strike. Where am I going to go every day, what am I going to do with all that sunshine?

SHOT BY A MONKEY, Elsa leaned against the banyan, held a bandage to the wound. They'd entered camp just before dawn, made off with a pistol, some candy bars, and a Desmond Morris book. We counted as six shots rang out, one of them finding poor Elsa's arm. Relieved that the simian was out of ammunition, we packed up. On the way out of camp we noticed a monkey on the riverbank, hammering at a snake with the gun.

THE NORWOOD, a shoebox strip-mall bar out in the West Valley, open 6 A.M.–2 A.M., no Happy Hour. I park the rig out back and go in. It's dark and moist, walls bent, the floor slippery, like being inside the body of a slow-moving animal. I have my lunch of shooters and short beers and wait for Celia to bring the cartons of cigarettes that I sell back at the plant. I don't smoke.

HIS CHUTE FAILED TO OPEN and as he fell he struck a pigeon, pinning it against his chest as they rushed toward the ground in tandem. He felt the pigeon's heart beating against his own. He closed his eyes and imagined he had two hearts, one outside his body and one inside, beating like a train.

I CORK HER NAVEL with a ruby, bring her saffron and pomegranates, dates, and cool water from the well. We sit together on the balcony, silk cushions beneath us. The air smells of jasmine from the gardens. We gaze out at the sea. A fisherman is pulling in his nets, back bent and straining, his catch nothing but seaweed and bad luck. I pour tea.

HE WAS HANDCUFFED to the seat beneath the window. He leaned out and tipped his hat to her with his free hand. She smiled and left the station platform. What a nice young man, she thought. The cats wove around her ankles when she opened the door. They reminded her of a painting of two golden fish she had seen in a picture book about Japan. They were on a green background, one facing up, the other down, nose to tail. Japan, imagine that.

I READ somewhere that Hitler loved dogs, was sentimental, too. Now, I'm a sucker for a hound, and a Charlie Rich song can fog up my glasses, so I started in to wondering about myself, you know, like deep down, could I maybe have mass murderer tendencies or something? Then I read he believed in astrology and felt a whole lot better, 'cause I'm a good Baptist. And also, I'm a Virgo, and we are very focused in our beliefs.

THE SERVANTS SEEM PECULIAR lately. The kitchen help, the housekeeper, and the gardener move about in a shuffle, mumbling, glazed. When I confront them they appear startled, as if just awakened. Only Claude, the chauffeur, retains his old demeanor, sneering or scowling, smoking a Gauloises as he leans against the Packard, wiping a long black fender with my cashmere sweater.

STUMBLE was our first line of defense when the cops swept the blocks. With one leg shorter than the other, he was an easy grab. The rest of us ran for our hidey-holes and waited it out while the popo twisted Stumble's arm and laid his face open. They broke a couple of his teeth once so he was known as Mumble for a while. Ma hated the nicknames so at home I had to call him Randolph.

I QUIT the vinyl-siding gig . . . that guy was an ass-hole. My lucky day . . . got a job at a bait and tackle shop. What I know about fishing you could fit on the side of a rubber worm, but the owner said I look like a pirate and I know how to make change, so the tourists'll be happy. If Gina wears a bikini and sits in the window, he'll pay extra.

MICK JAGGER BLEW HIS NOSE into the scarf hanging around his neck; our time together was coming to a close. I had my story after a week on the road discussing women and drugs and blues and shoes. Keith was jealous, said Mick never talked shoes with him. Charlie yawned, picked his teeth with a gold tie-pin, wiped it on Keith's shirt and returned it to its place — piercing a lovely puce and chartreuse regimental tie.

"WANT A SANDWICH? I got baloney, cheese, some of that Jewish bread." He still wore an apron in the kitchen, like a short-order cook, but couldn't peel an onion. I drew a bunny on the steamed-up window and followed the drips to the sill, looked into the yard where Ronnie used to chase me with a stick. It was full of gray snow, a couple of animal dents. "No, I ain't got time. I just dropped by, see how you were doing."

I'M THE ONLY DADDY in the carpool. Carpool Daddy. When it's my turn to drive, I want to kiss each Mommy and give her ass a little squeeze, tell her to have a nice day, that I can't wait to see her in the evening when I get home. The kid gets in the car, I pull away and watch Mommy in the rearview mirror. I memorize what she's wearing as she waves to us before going back inside.

SHE WAS BEAUTIFUL, fragile and afraid, a peacock in a hailstorm. We sat together on the couch, waiting for the car horn. It sounded at last and I held her hand as we pushed through the snow in the driveway. I turned away after I buckled her into the back seat. Don wouldn't look at me, but reached back, touched her knee. I watched them drive off, then walked back to the house, careful not to step into her footprints.

THERE IS A DEEP HOLE where the lies go. Not just downright falsehoods, but misaligned intentions, omissions of truth, innuendos, and the like. And don't go nosying up for a look-see, hear? Because there's a hand that will come up, quick as THAT! and grab your ankle or your coattail, see? And it won't let go, you'll be captive. And it won't let go, oh no no no.

WE ARE ON A RIDGE overlooking their encampment. Only women and children, the old and infirm, remain; the men are gone hunting or raiding. As I draw my saber and point it at the camp, I see the reflection of my horse's wild eye in the shiny metal. He knows there will be fire and screaming, the smell of blood and smoke before he can drink from the river.

KISS ME A QUESTION, ask me again with your eyes and I'll answer with my fingers, trailing reasons down your spine. There's a theory behind your knees and a postulate in that sweet spot on your neck, and I'll respond to your query with a smooch and a holler, roll you up against the sink and wash your hair, make love till the plates fall off the shelf.

THE HOTEL WAS ON FIRE, the guests marooning out front in evening clothes, pajamas, wrapped in towels. The building was saved from major damage by an efficient and powerful overhead extinguisher system that also managed to ruin furniture and clothes and TVs and books and laptops. A sprinkler intervention took place in room 807 as I spread an ounce of coke on the table.

I HAD AN IDEA that lasted more than four hours. I called my doctor. He said it should be removed. I said that's a good idea. He said: "Which? Your idea or the removal?" I said: "I have no idea." He said: "Fine, then we'll bill your insurance."

I HAD NEVER used a chain saw. When I plunged it into the neck of the tree it stuck, and I pulled hard, fell backwards. The saw sliced off part of my scalp, deli style, on the way down, then sputtered, scuttled away like a mad crab. I passed out, woke later to a low growl. Lucky was lapping at the pool of blood next to my head. I was glad to see him, his yellow eyes.

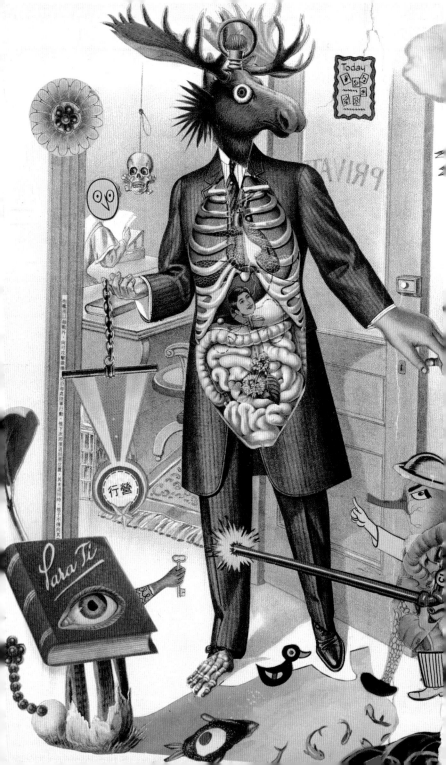

THE ROAD CLUTCHES at the side of the mountain as if it's afraid of falling. Narrow and rocky, it winds up the eastern slope as the engine labors and gripes about the load. The exhaust mingles with the smell of the sea, which is beyond our view. Paul and I are hauling lumber to Norma's camp and will build her cabin, give her the chance to measure our worth, each of us hoping not to be the one who drives back down alone.

ANN O'DYNE, nurse, had healing hands, wee mitts sprung from the cuffs of her crisp white tunic. Her voice was gold, a brook in a meadow. It washed away fear and anger, discomfort and pain. She was the pride of the ward, the whole hospital, the surgeon's pal, the patient's savior. At home, her feet hurt, she drank, slept with a butcher, called talk-radio programs, ranted about illegal immigrants and the Jew-run media.

I LIVE IN THE POCKET of a bright paisley shirt — silk — and when the light is just so, I'm in my own private cathedral. I lie back and push out against the fabric with my feet, and the colored light falls in like kids' breakfast cereal. I lived in a canvas shirt once but the guy was always sweating so much it recalled that tent in Ireland near the sea where I first got this assignment.

IN '98 Pasker and I subcontracted to paint a suspension bridge that spanned the M'pozo River in Congo. One day while adjusting the compressor we saw thirty or forty paramilitary guys running our way with machetes and AK-47s. We were terrified, but as they got closer they began to laugh, pointing at the spreading wet stain on the front of Pasker's pants, and ran past us. Once again, Pasker had saved our lives.

THERE WAS A MAN on my lawn. I saw him through the window. He was sitting with his legs straight out in front of him, hands in lap, back very erect. I armed myself with a baseball bat, went outside. "What are you doing here?" I said. He smiled and said: "I am Right Angle Man." Relieved that he was harmless, I laughed, said: "Where is your cape?" He looked up at me. "I am not a superhero. Are you with the Yankees?"

I RISE at 3 A.M. to walk my bladder to the bathroom, then return to bed and wait for my face and pillow to come to an agreement. I lie on my right, my left, my stomach, my back, as if attempting an even tan, until I find the Goldilocks spot. The only sound is the hum of the planet, and the whistling and chirping of the little birds who live in my nostrils.

THE NURSE LEFT. Ann's eyes were closed so I dumped her meds into my shirt pocket, snapped it shut. I looked around the room, put her laptop in my backpack. I leaned over to give her a goodbye peck on the forehead. She smelled like her next bath was going to be in the Ganges. Her eyes flew open, she grabbed my wrist and said: "Ronnie, give me a smoke."

THERE IS A PLACE I visit, where no one else goes. The rocks are slippery and sharp, the drop to the dark sea below makes me dizzy. The sun never muscles its way through the gang of clouds that hover overhead, shedding a mist that plasters my thin hair to my head, makes me turn up my collar. No, you can't go with me, I don't want a sandwich to take, thermos of hot chocolate, though your asking may keep me home.

SHE LOVED SECRETS, stole magazines, makeup, sauntered through the office pulling at the hem of her sweater, hiding her hips. Her hands were pudgy and dainty, dimpled like a doll's, always used a paper napkin to hold her fried chicken. "Hello, Jerome," she purred as I put down my briefcase, hung up my coat, "what's on YOUR agenda today?" "Regulators coming in." "I can help!" she said. "I can help."

THE RHUBARB grows in wild patches against the wooden fence separating our backyard from that of Mrs. Bonkowski next door. I snap a stalk and dip it in sugar, gnaw and suck on it until my teeth hurt. Divisions of plastic army men engage in battle with pill bugs and earwigs in the rhubarb forest, the dirt on my knees and elbows testimony to the conflict. A truce is called for dinner; peace prevails.

THERE'S A GLASS on the nightstand, a smear of lipstick along the rim. It is empty. On the dresser, an assortment of bracelets, earrings, her wedding band, a framed photo of her father in uniform. There is a stain on the bedspread, peeking out from beneath the suitcase that lies open, ready to receive. She pulls hard at the closet door, which has stuck ever since they moved here. He's never gotten around to fixing it.

SHINBONE AND NUSBAUM sit in a rear booth facing the door, able to see whoever walks in. They are patient, serious, comfortable sitting for long stretches eating pie and drinking cold coffee. Shinbone looks at Nusbaum. "Hey, Nussy, you heard about the Jew what fell offa Hoover Dam?" Nusbaum picks something out of his cup, flicks it at the window, where it splats and slides to the sill. "Shut up, Bone," he says.

THE TRAIN pulls into Jawbone at 1:07. I'm on the platform waiting for you but the only passengers off the car are three old farmers. I stand there for a while, look around, hoping you'll appear out of the heat. The engine chugs off into the dust and I retreat to the Red Dog, drink until I'm numb, then stumble past the livery barn to lie down on the tracks. I put my ear to the rail, close my eyes and listen for you.

"DON'T DRINK the tap water," she said with science in her eyes. I ran out the back door to the fields and started husking. I was overwhelmed with affection for the kernels festooning the shucked ears. I lay down between the stalks, pressed my face to the deep soft earth and inhaled. There is no other life.

I CAN'T HEAR YOU, my thumb's up my ass. The phone is ringing, someone's at the door. I'm not getting up. Don't bother writing. Sure — call whomever you want. Gather your friends and stir some stink, I have lace hankies. You drive to work and buy cans of beans, mark an X where told, your pages are numbered. I don't have to listen. I own the ocean.

CRAWFOOT stood outside of Sloans, hand up for a cab. His face was punctuated by a cigar, and a redhead hung on his arm like a comma. He'd approached her after his third Dewars and water. "You make a barstool look like a throne." She looked him over, suppressed a smile. "Yeah? You make wearing a raincoat look like a felony." He lit her cigarette, loosened his tie and sat down next to her, bumped her knee.

EXPL   EL.

THE OTHERS are already on Main. I'm still here looking for my hat. I search everywhere and finally find it in your closet. I rush out and jump on Bucky, his flank rippling with anticipation. We get in formation just as the band starts booming and we strut down the street. The riders wave to the crowd, smiles all around. I see you up ahead on the platform, next to the mayor, and something starts to hurt in my chest.

THE ELEVATOR IS BROKEN. I lug a bag of groceries up the metal stairs to the eighth floor. Half-way there the soggy bottom of the bag breaks, releases a fusillade of cat food cans that go clanking and bouncing below. I sigh and sit, feel as empty as the bag. I stare at the white curdles of cottage cheese from the burst container, now on my shoes, and think this is what angel vomit must look like.

A BIRD LIVES ON MY HEAD, nests in my hair, pecks at my scalp. A finch, I believe. When I go out in public I cover it with a hat, so it's away from prying eyes and cats who would climb my body to catch it. Sometimes on the bus I notice others wearing hats, and if there are seeds or an errant feather on their shoulders, I nod and smile and preen.

WE WERE on a tour boat in Boston Harbor. A candy wrapper escaped from some kid's hand, scuttled our way across the deck. Russell pinned it with his boot, bent over, picked it up. A gust of wind snatched it from him, sent it out over the water. An old woman said: "Shame on you, littering." My brother's neck went red. He got that look that could clear a barroom in Quincy. He sighed, winked at me. "Yes, ma'am," he said.

HER MOUTH is a hammer. I kiss it and fall, pummeled, to the floor, crawl to my corner and rest. She summons me later to mix a drink, plait her hair, massage her feet. I am clumsy — she cuts my cheek with a toenail, presses her big toes into my eye sockets. I lie there shamed, foot-faced and humbled, her all-natural organic toy, and wait.

I SIT IN THIS ROOM in the castle's turret and fashion animals out of twigs and string. I stop and get up from my stool and look out the window. I can see the fortress wall and the farmlands and orchards and the sea beyond, and at times, a ship on the water. When it rains, I can only see as far as the farmlands, where an ox stands still in the downpour. Just as it does when the sky is clear.

I WAKE with headache. Anchored at my eyebrows, it spreads back like the tentacles of a jellyfish to sting and poison my brain. It hurts to see, everything the color of smokers' teeth. I close my eyes, full of sand. My ears enroll a hum, a steady electric signal from the past, a history lesson I can't make out. My fingers are lead soldiers, stripped of paint, heavy and dull. Hello! I must be dying. My chin is a stump.

THE FIRE AND SMOKE drive me to the window. Only a two-story drop, but I'm sure to break my leg if I hit the ground. I start my new gig at the Ice Capades next week (Snoopy) and I don't want to jeopardize it. If I can land on the awning of the grocery next door it might break my fall. I leap and hit the awning, tear through it and collapse onto a crate of tomatoes. Mrs. Liu runs out. "Hello, Tony," she says and claps her hands.

THE SKY — blue, flat, clear — sits on a hard horizon below which is green meadow puckered with yellow flowers, filling the bottom of the frame. In the smack center sits a red chair, wood unadorned, vibrating against the blue and green. A black bird lights on the seat, shits a splotch of white, departs on the diagonal. A painting.

HIS HANDS jump into the bowl, the ground meat, to join the conversation going on with the raw egg, onions, the salt and pepper. He squeezes it all through his fingers and wonders if his brain would feel like this if he grabbed it from behind. Cooking calms him, makes him introspective. This is Life, he thinks. You put a lot of stuff together, smoosh it around, and pretty soon you've got a bunch of meatballs.

HE SAID the questions were merely routine, the sort always asked during a homicide investigation. He kept looking at my shoes, then over my shoulder into the kitchen where I kept knives on a magnetic board, the points always up. The wet rags on the floor seemed to interest him. I invited him in, asked if he'd like some coffee, look at an album of photographs, some of which showed the slain neighbor wearing pajamas.

"THE NEW swim coach is really nice, Daddy. He likes to give my neck and shoulders a massage when I get out of the pool." She smiles at me, her hair still wet. "Do you know the phone number of the PE Department at school?" I say. "Oh, can we invite him over for dinner?" I put the phone down. "Do your homework. Daddy's going out for a while."

"WHAT'CHA WANNA go on a game show for?" She was disinclined to answer, thought it obvious, but said, "To win money and prizes and shit." She ran a wet finger around the rim of her glass, couldn't make it sing. He continued ironing the napkins. "You gonna wear a costume?" She turned slowly, found his eyes hovering in the iron's steam, stared until he looked away. "I do not intend to make a fool of myself."

I WENT TO HIGH SCHOOL WITH THE KING. Well, actually he was a grade ahead, but I'd see him in the halls surrounded by his bodyguards disguised as varsity football players, as if no one knew who he was, for crissakes. He always arrived late and left early, sat alone in the cafeteria. I felt sorry for him and one time approached him at lunch, offered him my sweet roll. He said something in French, then closed his eyes.

SHE WAS INDISCRIMINATE in her taste for jewelry. Paste, carats, costume, it was all glam flocking. She was like a magpie, hoarding sparkles in a box. Every day she put on earrings, necklaces, brooches, bangles, bracelets, and pins, none of which matched; an upended Christmas display held together by some hair and a dress from the bottom of a closet with a burned-out light.

THE LONG CARGO SHIP pulls itself across the ocean and comes to rest at the port. In the morning it stands upright on its hind legs and with resolve heads toward the business district and settles into the middle of the block. It removes its raincoat and folds it, puts it on the roof of the community center, then opens its doors to share the wares that braved the waves. This is Legend. This is IKEA.

I STOLE a car once, a Buick Riviera that had a dent in the door, a puckered triangle where the paint went all funny. I used to steal a lot of things back then, magazines, school supplies, cigarettes, clothes, beer. I work downtown now, have a family, am an honest citizen. Yesterday I saw that long-ago car in a lot, touched the wounded door and felt a rush of joy, an awareness of a heavenly Fagin watching over me.

LITTLE FLUFF knocks over the dish of milk. "Naughty, naughty," says Mother Kitty. "You may not go out to play." Little Fluff begins to cry. Mother Kitty wipes her tears and says: "If you promise to be more careful in the future, you may join your friends outside." Little Fluff promises and runs outside, where Mitsy and Binks are setting fire to some trash and smoking the marijuana cigarette.

HER FEROCITY left him indisposed to fight back and finally to even listen. She squinted, eyed him like a pot of boiling water watches a raw egg. She filled the salt shaker. "What's the matter, Jerome?"

JESSE PAINTED a face on a rock and threw it into the pond in August, when the water was warm and buzzed over by flies and bees. It lay trapped in the silt at the bottom, stared up at the sky, waited for Jesse to appear overhead in the old skiff. A stickleback swam by, came back, puzzled by the face, then darted after a light mote, hoping for a meal. Jesse was away that summer and the face dissolved, was just a rock.

SHE SHOWED HIM THE TIES in the case, and as she bent down he studied the top of her head, wanted to sniff it. He imagined her as his lover, meeting in her cheap but cheerful apartment, far from his large home. She would cook him meals her Italian grandmother had taught her to make and he would tell her lies about his childhood. He bought three ties, paid cash, and never shopped there again.

"SHUT UP," he says. Being playful, she thinks, things being pretty steady between them lately. She holds his hand, huge, the knuckles like walnuts under the skin and smelling of machinery. He's a pressman at the *Times*, and when he comes home at night tired, she unlaces his heavy boots, pushes him back onto the couch and lays against his overalls, so that when they go to bed later they both smell of oil, and ink.

RAY WAS THIS TENOR PLAYER, good tone, good hands, never played with the big guys, but still, he was good. Between sets Ray would take out some Silly Putty, you know, that kids' stuff, and stretch it and pull it and even make little animals and things. Said it kept his fingers limber. In his pockets he'd carry three or four of those plastic eggs the stuff came in. That's how he come to have the nickname the Hen.

THE SKY is sullen and agnostic. The sea roams for color, any green or blue. The shore lays swollen, a drunken whore, covered with plastic bottles, the surf her snore. I walk, search for salvage, anything to sell. I spot a small coin that looks like a dime — it is a Czech koruna. I've found Prague in a dune, rush home to prepare for my journey. "Find anything?" you say. "Nope," I say and stomp the sand from my boots.

SHE WAS FROM TRINIDAD. She was beautiful. She lived upstairs from the dry cleaner on Third Avenue. I loved her. All that winter I pestered my mother did she need me to take something to the cleaners. She said we never used no dry cleaner except that one time, my sister's Communion dress. So I applied for a job at the cleaners and the lady there smiled and said: "Sugar, you are too, too young."

I OPEN THE CAN, press the oil out of the tuna with the lid. I recall sandwiches you made, just the right amount of mayo, onions, celery, sourdough with lettuce or, if you were happy, alfalfa sprouts. In my reverie I don't notice that I've sliced my thumb with the lid and blood mingles with the oil and flows down the drain and pipes to a processing plant and to sea, to finally wash up on a beach where we once fished.

"DO YOU believe in God?" The trunk lid blocks the view of his face. My hands are bound, and I am pressed against the spare tire. If there was a God, I would believe in him. The lid comes down and I am in darkness. It smells of oil and gas and rubber.

SHE SAT on the porch in the old rocker, back and forth, back and forth, tried to puzzle out her feelings. The paperboy hit her in the knee with the *Times*. She kept on rocking. Kids ran by, the UPS truck rumbled past, a dog shat on her lawn. She just kept rocking, thinking. The sun went down, cars pulled into driveways. Her husband climbed the steps. "Hi, hon." He put down his briefcase. "Fuck you, Larry!" she said.

I WAKE UP naked except for the socks on my feet, and shoes. The shoes do not belong to me, the socks a type I would never wear. There is a crowbar in the bed with something pooled on the sheet beneath it, dark and sticky to the touch. I try to remove the shoes but I cannot undo the laces, they have been triple-knotted, tight as stretched skin. I am afraid to stand up.

OH, he was proud, all right, people slapped his back, wanted his picture. He'd worked very hard on the saddle, designed it himself, the tooling, the conchos. It was being shipped in from Tulsa by train, would arrive any day. Yet he could already feel himself withdrawing from it, sensed its luster fading, his joy dwindling. He'd had the same feeling on the day he married Emilene, confetti all around, her hair shiny.

AFTER the unfortunate, some might say unnatural, occurrence between Claude and Clothilde — our cook of many years — in the pantry, I suspended only Claude for a fortnight. We have to eat, after all. Après bidet this morning, I stood on the terrace, gazed upon the sheep flocking the expanse of lawn, keeping it trim, and decided to let Claude go permanently, then went down to the pantry.

THE LIGHTS are hotter than I thought they'd be. I sit in the guest chair and they adjust my microphone, pat the sweat off my forehead, ask if I'd like a glass of water. "Two minutes," says the floor manager. My heart is pounding. I run from the stage to the bathroom and vomit until I'm empty. I find the nearest exit, push it open, set off the alarm. I lean against a statue, press my head against the cool bronze leg.

IRIS BEDLICK sang backup. Country, soul, rock, whatever, had a voice could shatter a glass or put a baby to sleep. One night, on the road with Jack Howlette, she was handed a drink that blistered her throat. She never sang again, turned her back on music, was last heard to be a hotel maid. Her replacement married Jack, divorced him, went solo, platinum albums, a Grammy. Started out a chemistry major, became a star.

A PORCH at the back of my head. A bird on the railing. In the sun at the bottom of the stairs lies a dog named Perfect. His muzzle flutters as he breathes, soft, sleepy. I don't go there often, too busy up front. When I do sit, eyes closed, feet up on the rail, I smell grass, dirt, the river. I hear the mountain as it inches forward, pulling the rest behind until it meets itself, breaks into a grin, shakes the ocean into a fountain.

SHE LOVED HIM and Valentine's Day, but she adored chocolate. He knew all this yet stood before her in his white terry robe empty-handed, no heart-shaped box, no Godiva bag, nothing from Richart or Maison du Chocolat, nothing from Belgium, not a hint of bonbons stuffed with truffles or hazelnut pyramids filled with nougatine. "OK, where is it?" she said. He smiled and pushed her down on the bed. "You'll see," he said.

RONNIE smacks the bar, tries to topple the splendid tower of quarters I've erected in front of me, but it just leans a bit toward my warm beer. He says I'm gilding my misery, playing all those weepers on the jukebox by Ray Price and George Jones. He tries mitigating with Def Leppard and Lynyrd Skynyrd, but ain't no rock 'n' roll can ease the pain of losing my sweet Junie Bird.

I LAY THE BOOK on the floor, open to the middle. It's a lovely volume, green leather covers, engraved endpapers. I remove my shoes and step into it up to my ankles, knees, hips, chest, until only my head is showing and the pages spread around me and the words bob up and down and bump into my neck, and the punctuation sticks to my chin and cheeks so I look like I need a shave.

EDDIE FORMED his hand, fingers, into the shape of a duck's head. "Whaddya wanna do today, Bill?" he said. "Let's trim my nose hairs," said the hand. Eddie stood on a stool at the sink, turned on the water, the garbage disposal, began inching Bill into the dark maw of the drain. From the other room, Mother's voice: "Edward! What are you doing in there?" Eddie pulled back his hand, looked at Bill. "Nothin', Ma, nothin.'"

THE POND froze over last night, black pane frosted, framed by a stubble of cattail and brush. A blackbird sways on a stalk of swamp weed, the red and yellow patch on his shoulder his rank, little corporal. Geese fly overhead, big V honking south. Jesse and I bring the old skiff back to the barn. She wants to buy some red paint, give the boat a facelift. I say why spend the money, we've got gray paint right here.

VERA "WOOLY" LAMB dressed like a man, and could outcuss, outshoot, and outdrink anyone in pants, Little Rock, 1922. Her saloon, the Gilded Rose, offered games of chance and some local talent, girls from farms and factories tired of dirty work. Wooly kept a single-shot derringer tucked away on her person in a strategic spot hidden and moist, the humidity finally rendering the gun inoperative at a crucial moment.

THE BODY IN THE BACK SEAT looks familiar but I've been cautioned not to turn around. I only catch a glimpse when I look in the vanity mirror to see if any of the spinach manicotti that we had a while ago at Mangia has stuck to my teeth — I hate when I look like a mook. Gina turns up the radio when Slayer comes on, lights a cigarette, and sings along at the top of her voice, elbow out the window like a trucker, happy.

IN THE GRAY morning I arrive at the palace for questioning. Everything I've ever said or done, everywhere I've lived, everyone I've met or spoken to, is examined. My life is scrutinized; reduced, finally, to sunspots and murmurs. In a smoky room with yellow chairs I am found guilty as charged. I am sentenced to spend the rest of my days sifting through what they've allowed me to remember.

AFTER SHE FLED he became his own wife, ironing in his underwear, dusting the shelves, moving the figurines to the dining room table then replacing them carefully when he'd finished waxing the cabinet. Wearing her apron, he often made casseroles. Sometimes he'd sit on her closet floor and move his face through her dresses, like a dog searching in a field of high grass.

JOE PRINGLE, father of Sunday and six other children named after days of the week, rushed in and struck Mumford's skull with a sheep's head, still hot from the stockpot in the kitchen. One of the sheep's eyes popped out upon impact, as did one of Mumford's. They rolled under the table together, as if looking for the dogs that lay there waiting.

I FLAY my skin for you. It hangs from my chest and arms and back like a fringed jacket, like I'm going to a Neil Young concert, like I smell of patchouli and boo, like I stick to the seat of your VW. Except that the shreds have hardened and clink against one another. I'm a human wind chime. Hey man, can you hear me now?

IT WAS A LARGE SHIP. Growing from the main deck was a tall oak, its limbs reaching beyond the gunwales and casting a shadow on the water. At the very top sat a crow, keeping watch, while below him lesser whistlers and chirpers and screechers went about their duties, making sure the leaves were fit to cup the wind that pushed the great vessel through the sea.

HE WAITED all his life for a splashy catharsis, irrefutable evidence that a profound change had transformed him. It took him many years to realize that he had been altered each day by the sun's rising and the moon's movement, by the unfurling of his daughter's tiny hand to grasp his thumb, by the cat on his chest, by the glass of water his wife brought him before bedtime, by the questions his son asked.

"LET ME IN!" The failed artist from around the corner, 6 ft. 4 in. of canned ham, and his wee wife, 5 ft. 1, a regular pill bug, was banging on my door. A bird had just shit on his head, an avian comment on his life. Drug-riddled and depressed, he was making lots of money in the video game industry. "What should I do?" he asked. I thought he should shoot himself, but didn't say so. I handed him a towel.

GEORGE Man-Walking held a sweet feeling for Mary Trout and her dog, Reno. Three weeks on the road, he'd come by, bring her trinkets, keepsakes from his route, a red thermometer, odd buttons, a pin made of acorns, soap. He'd have a bag for Reno, too, some chop bones, bits of biscuit. Mary died one summer and George took Reno home, kept bringing trinkets to the dog, filled its little house with stuff until it ran away.

HER SUMMER DRESS is crisp, white with dark blue polka dots, open at the throat, sleeveless, set off by a wide red patent leather belt and espadrilles that raise her heels three inches from the sticky tarpaper. Backlit by the sun, her hair a splendor, she walks to the edge of the roof garden, looks down for a moment at the street sixty stories below, then returns to water the tomato plants. There are no insects up here.

THE CITY BELOW is brown and gray, some black smoke. The landing is smooth. I find a cab and take it to a street where old elms lean over small shops. I limp through the slush. The bell tinkles when I open the door and the barber turns from stropping the razor, nods toward a chair. I go to the photo on the wall. It's of three pilots, and I peer through my reflection at the man in the middle.

THEY BOUGHT apples, asked for directions. I didn't like their looks, the way the one in charge talked to the blonde in the back seat, ordered the driver around. I tried to recall where I left the pump gun. Annie put her hand on my arm, always able to read my mind. They drove off after eating some apples, threw the cores out the window. Annie thought maybe it was time to close up the stand, keep Fall just for ourselves.

I DROP IT INTO an athletic sock, the heavy kind with the double row of red bands around the top. I knot the sock and heave it as hard as I can into the lagoon and watch as an egret drops down to inspect the ripples. He stands on one leg and I realize the water is shallow, only comes halfway up his leg. "Shit!" I roll up my pants, remove my shoes, and wade into the muck.

ARDELLE PHELPS JR. drove to Lowburn, parked across from Buddy's just before closing time and waited. He recalled the good times he'd had with Faye, couldn't come up with any fresher than ten years old. Faye stumbled out of Buddy's, leaned on Erskine and laughed, took off her shoes. Ardelle checked himself in the rearview, made sure there wasn't anything stuck to his teeth, and slid out of the pickup.

HE SITS IN THE SUN rearranging the past, and tries to keep warm. He knows words, says them, but has forgotten their meaning. They hang all about, sparkling, just out of reach, the crystals on a chandelier he can't light. His memory rings like a wind chime, sounding clear and bright, then dwindles to random jingles and clinks.

I REMOVE MY HEADGEAR and glance out the porthole at Earth, slowly receding. I am elated, relieved to be leaving the riots and wars, fires, famines, and floods. Deep Colony 7 has new doctrines; things work, it is clean, there is Hope. I scratch inside the flight suit. I sniff my fingertips, light up a Marlboro and cough.

THEY'VE TAGGED my fence again with their gang squiggles, street-dumb calligraphy. They walk by on the way to school, I know who they are. I will sit in my pickup across the street every day, and wait with my own spray paint, shake the cans until my wrists hurt, catch them in the act. I'll jump out, the aerosol avenger, and cover their faces and backs with perfect penmanship, my name. You don't fuck with Jerry Vogel.

I WAS NEW, and scared. We were hunkered down behind a berm, taking heavy fire. Stein looked at me: "Fear is just another weapon, like your sidearm or grenade. You can use it to shoot yourself in the foot or blow up the platoon. Or you can turn it around and use it on the bad guys." Standing by his casket at the memorial a month later, I wondered if grief was a weapon, too.

WHEN I WAS TWELVE I took all the coins from my parents' change jar. I went down to the end of the street where the train tracks were and laid all the coins out on the rails and waited for the train. After it passed I gathered the flattened coins and brought them home and epoxied them to the coffee table. It was stunning! I was so very proud of my achievement. When my parents came home I was given a beating.

I WET my lips with the tip of my tongue, leave it protruding for a beat, reel it back in. Is she watching? She must know I do it for her. Is she watching? I sit up straight, order whiskey, no rocks. Is she watching? I laugh, make a joke. Is she watching? I walk to the men's room, saunter. Is she watching? I return, swing my leg over the back of the chair, knock over a bottle of beer. Damn, is she watching? Is she watching?

THERE IS A TURD on our wedding cake, a child's poop. Deirdre is weeping in the ladies' while I push through the guests looking for Sheila, that loser, the only one who would do such a thing, another one of her "messages" claiming I'm the father of her ugly baby. We spent one night together. One night! And no, I won't submit to a DNA thing . . . I don't do well on tests. There she is! Grab her, someone! Stop that woman!

THEY PUT ME IN A CHAIR, hand me a container of warm yogurt, a spoon. It is like eating flannel. They've forgotten to search my pockets, request that I stand. I don't feel like it, cross my arms to indicate my refusal. The gag doesn't allow me to tell them and hoisting my middle finger would be seen as combative, an excuse to use the prod. I get up, of course, and they find your picture. They pass it around and smirk.

THE BLOODLETTING commenced at first light. Swooping into their camp, we trampled and savaged all life before us, giving no thought or quarter to the age or gender of heathen. Some fought back, valiantly, admirably, I admit, while others cowered in their huts holding onto amulets as if some pagan god could protect them from our sabers. There was nothing of value in their sorry camp, and the women were not pleasing.

THE BRIDGE buckled and collapsed. Cars grill-smacked the river or hit trunk-first, springing hatches, spreading contents over the water — flip-flops, rope, plastic toys, funnels, tarps and bags from Trader Joe's, hats, bottles of sunscreen, cardboard boxes — in a yard-sale flotilla without buyers that drifted through the channel, then out to sea to join the rest of the shit in the ocean.

THERE IS A TERRIBLE ROCK in his chest. It burns and pushes. He waits for it to bloom. He knows that to grow wings he must kill everyone downstairs. He gets up and removes his socks, looks for his knife. He stands at the top of the stairs and takes deep breaths. He can already feel the wings pushing through his skin.

WHEN I DIE there will be no burial or cremation. I have contracted with Spacemetery® to store my remains aboard an Eterna satellite. My body will forever loop around the planet and emit a flashing light whenever it passes over a memorable location. Like that bar in Redondo Beach where we first met, or IKEA.

YEARNING for insight, some spiritual pointer, I lie amidst the shattered pieces of mirror and bleed. I had stumbled home drunk and, mistaking my reflection for an intruder, rushed at it, split my forehead, smashed the glass, fell to the floor. I turned my head and saw that the shards reflected the ceiling. I realized then that what is whole above is mirrored in broken pieces below.

HE DISMOUNTED at the dead end of the canyon, took a shovel and walked to a spot near a cottonwood and began to dig. When he was knee-deep in the hole, an arrow passed behind his head. He felt the air move and thought it a daring bird. The second arrow found its mark in his neck and the life seeped from him and he folded, inches from some letters and a lock of hair.

THE SEA is under the sky. The clouds are in the sky. The sun is between the clouds. My keys are on the table. I will be in the car, driving beneath the sky, toward the sea. There is a small house on the beach. The door is red. I will open the door and put my keys on the table. You will be in the blue chair near the window. You will turn, fold the corner of the page in the book you are reading, and rise to kiss me now.

HOT IN THE BAIT SHOP today. Guy walks in, all big city, Jew hair, glasses. I'm thinking, only thing he's ever fished for is a compliment. "Can I help you?" "Yes, would you happen to carry any Yamamoto 9S Senko freshwater lures in a four inch?" Man, I felt like there was shit on my shoe. The dude was DEEP.

THE RAVEN SWAYS in the wind at the very top of the pine, a lone black pennant, an ensign signaling to those who watch that a storm is imminent. The wheat will boil, the saplings fold and snap. We close the barn doors and soothe the stalled horses with whispers and hands. A crack of thunder sends a shudder through them that passes into us, and we stand together grounded, all legs trembling.

YEARS BACK the river overflowed, flooded a nearby apple orchard. Grandpa was sitting on the high front porch watching the water rushing down the street when he saw a flotilla of apples bobbing past. He quick got his waders and proceeded to fish for fruit. Grandma made pies and applesauce and fritters for weeks. That's how the local saying "When the river rises, make fritters" come about. That's the origin, true story.

THE ORCHARD reminds me of Christmas, the trees hung with shiny round fruit. Pawel and I walk the long rows, remark on squirrels and birds we see, the bees. He tells of his father, found face-down in a creek nearby, arm broken, foot caught in a root. "What happened?" I say. "He wished for a better life." A jet flies overhead and Pawel falls to the ground, twists his leg beneath him, screams. "What happened?" I say.

ACKNOWLEDGMENTS

I am grateful to Will Amato, who helped me realize the value of these stories; to Ed Ward for being gracious enough to introduce me to his agent; to that agent, David Dunton, for helping secure the publication of this book; and to Tom Bouman, my editor, for his sound advice and enthusiasm.

A tip of the hat is also in order to Dave Alvin, Jeff Bridges, and Ian McShane for their exceptional generosity in recording some of these tales for the book's website, as well as to Jonathan Lethem, J. Robert Lennon, Joe Frank, Terry Gilliam, and Gary Panter for their kind words and encouragement. Many thanks to good neighbor Pete Sepenuk.

This book would not have been possible without Facebook and the many fans and followers of my writing there. I am most indebted to them.

And of course, Issa.